By Jennifer Liberts Weinberg
Illustrated by Carlo LoRaso and John Kurtz

First published by Parragon in 2012
Parragon
Queen Street House
4 Queen Street
Bath BA1 1HE, UK
www.parragon.com

ISBN 978-1-4454-4742-1

Printed in China

DUMBO

Fly, Dumbo, Fly!

A little story for little learners

Bath · New York · Singapore · Hong Kong · Cologne · Delhi
Melbourne · Amsterdam · Johannesburg · Auckland · Shenzhen

Peekaboo.

Who are you?

Dumbo!

"Achoo!"

Oh, dear.
Big ears.

A parade!

Oh, dear.

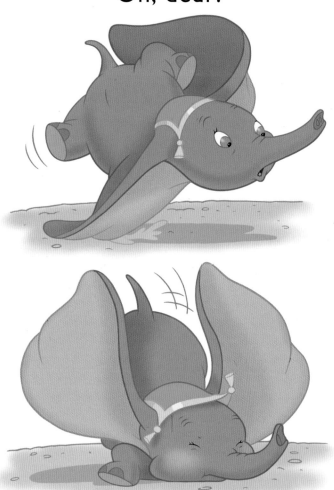

Those ears!

Poor Dumbo.

Who is there?

Timothy Q. Mouse.

"Cheer up, Dumbo!"

Friends!

Aha!

Wings!

"Jump, Dumbo!"

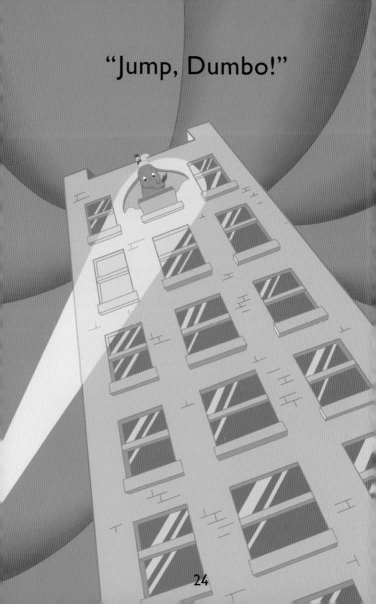

Down, down, down.

"Fly, Dumbo, fly!"
Dumbo tries.

Up, up, up.
Dumbo flies!

29